THIS
LITTLE
PIGGY

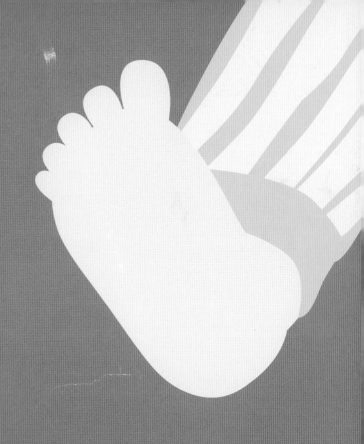

Balzer + Bray
An Imprint of HarperCollinsPublishers

THIS LITTLE PIGGY

By **Tim Harrington**

This little piggy went to market.

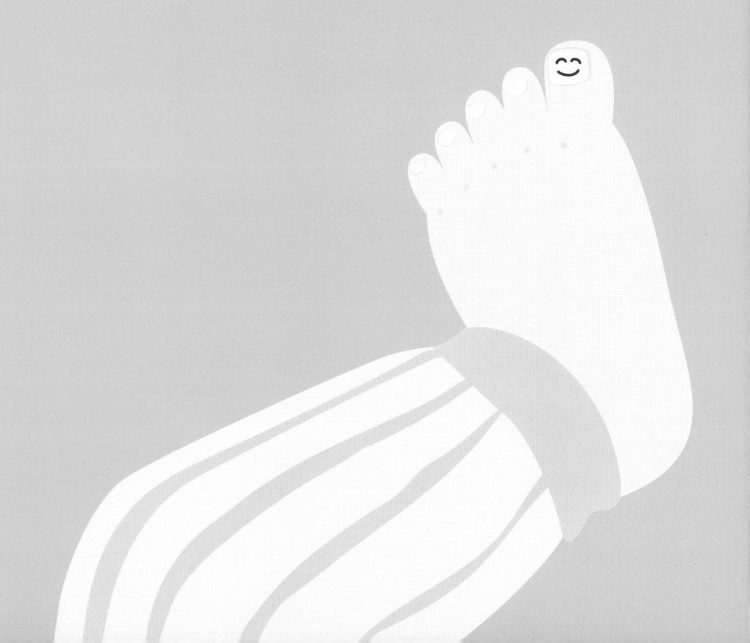

This little piggy stayed home.

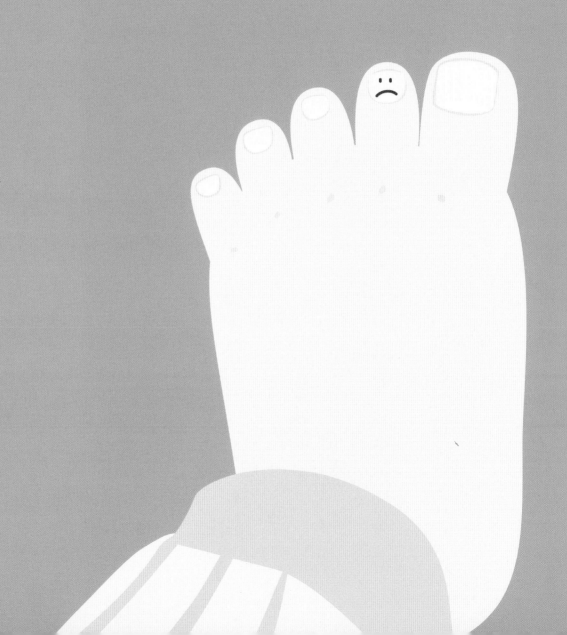

This little piggy had roast beef.

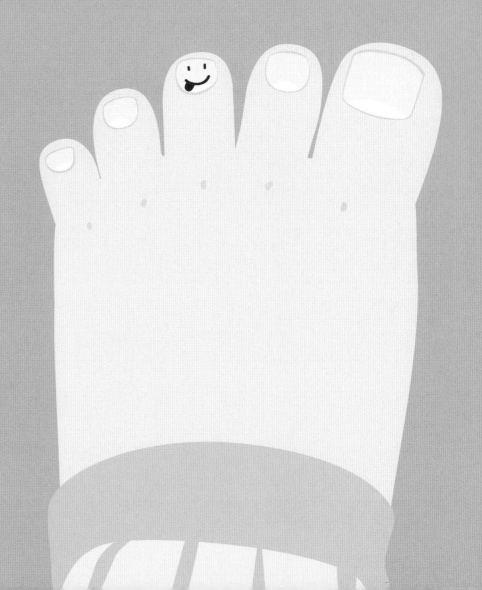

But this little piggy had none.

This little piggy went WEE! WEE! WEE! All the way home.

BUT!

On the other foot . . .

this little piggy dug dancing.

And this little piggy flew planes.

This little piggy sold hot dogs.

This little piggy loved paints.

This little piggy built a spaceship and flew to outer space, where he found a planet of green jelly creatures that taught him how to eat Martian marshmallows and play gravity tag and catch asteroid beetles. He started a successful robot repair shop, and on days off he rode the solar slides. Wee! Wee! Wee! All the way down!

All those crazy piggies made the market-visiting, roast beef–enjoying, wee-weeing piggies want to do more fun stuff too.

SO....

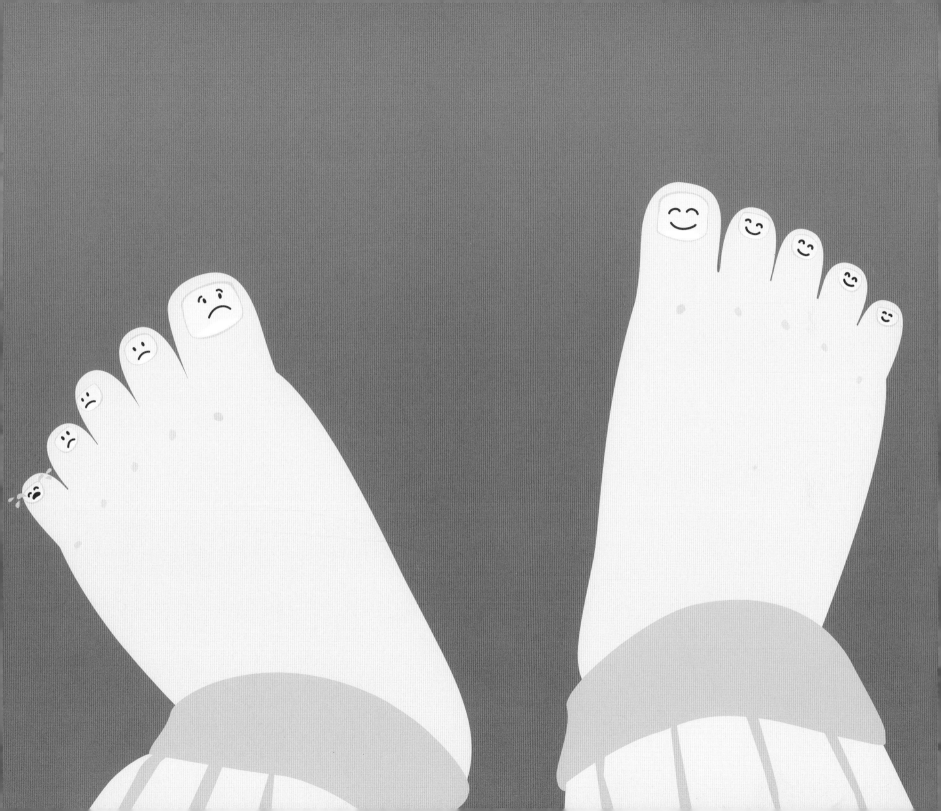

this little piggy had a costume party.

And this little piggy chewed gum.

This little piggy raced go-karts.

And this little piggy played drums.

This little piggy was secretly Super Toe, the world's greatest hero! Faster than a race car, he could blow out birthday candles from a mile away and fly high above the clouds. Once, he saved a leaky tugboat with a super bubble. And when a giant smelly sock attacked the city, Super Toe used Tickle Power to send it tee, hee, hee all the way home!

HAPPY BIRTHDAY
SUPER TOE!

Which is why now all
the little piggies
are just totally tired out
and really want a
good night's sleep.
SO....

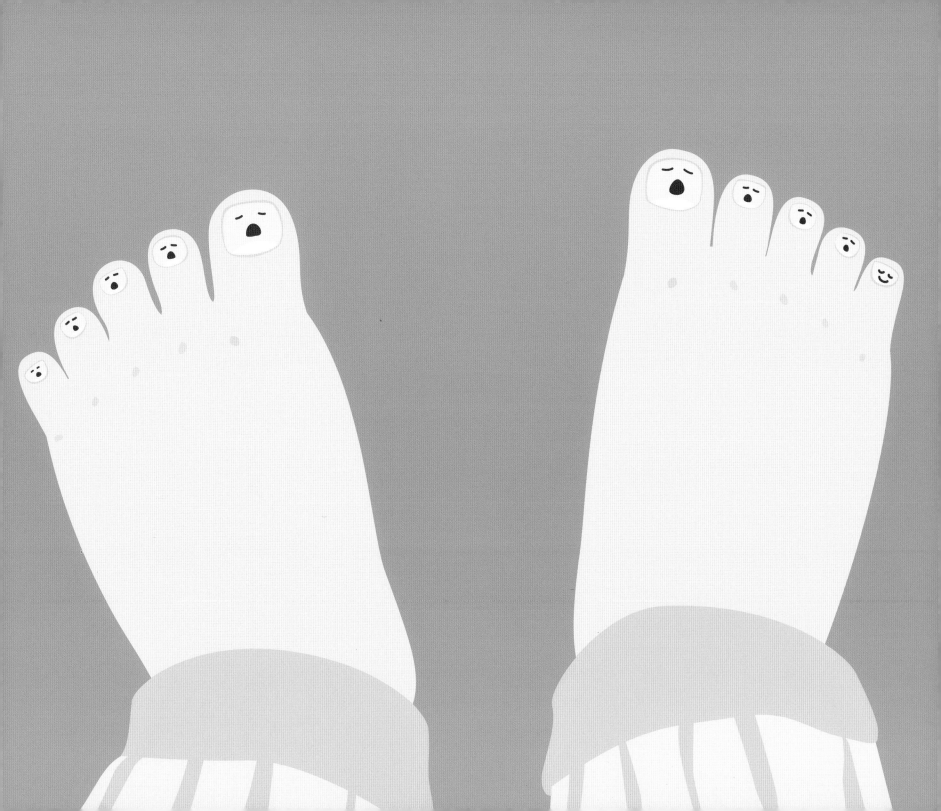

this little piggy's all dozy.

This little piggy gets clean.

This little piggy reads stories.

This little piggy brushes his teeth.

And this little piggy goes Z-z-z . . .

all the way to sleep.

For Benji's and Caspi's
delicious toes

Balzer + Bray is an imprint of HarperCollins Publishers. This Little Piggy. Copyright © 2013 by Tim Harrington. All rights reserved. Manufactured in China. No part of this book may be used or reproduced in any manner whatsoever without written permission except in the case of brief quotations embodied in critical articles and reviews. For information address HarperCollins Children's Books, a division of HarperCollins Publishers, 10 East 53rd Street, New York, NY 10022. www.harpercollinschildrens.com

Library of Congress Cataloging-in-Publication Data is available. ISBN 978-0-06-221808-7

The artist scanned his pencil-on-paper drawings and used Adobe Illustrator to create the digital artwork for this book.
Typography by Dana Fritts. 13 14 15 16 17   SCP   10 9 8 7 6 5 4 3 2 1 ❖ First Edition